To:

From: Author

Next time you see the rain smile
and be grateful!

Love,

_____

HetHeru AnkhBaRa

A Healing Blue
Lotus Book

Rain Please Stay

Published August 18, 2016, by the author -HetHeru AnkhBaRa

Printed in the United States of America.

ISBN-13: 978-1541189102

ISBN-10: 1541189108

HEALING BLUE LOTUS
HETHERU ANKHBARA
P.O. BOX 814
CENTRAL ISLIP, N.Y. 11722
healingbluelotus.com
718.314.4492

Dedicated

With LOVE, I dedicate this book to lovely TefNut; all the good aspects of Nature, and to my amazing children. I Love you.

-HetHeru AnkhBaRa

TefNut

This Book Belongs To:

_____

Rain
Please Stay

By

**HetHeru
AnkhBaRa**

Illustrated
by

Peipei

Rain, rain don't go away.

Please, please, please stay.

For as long as you can, you cool me down on a hot summer day.

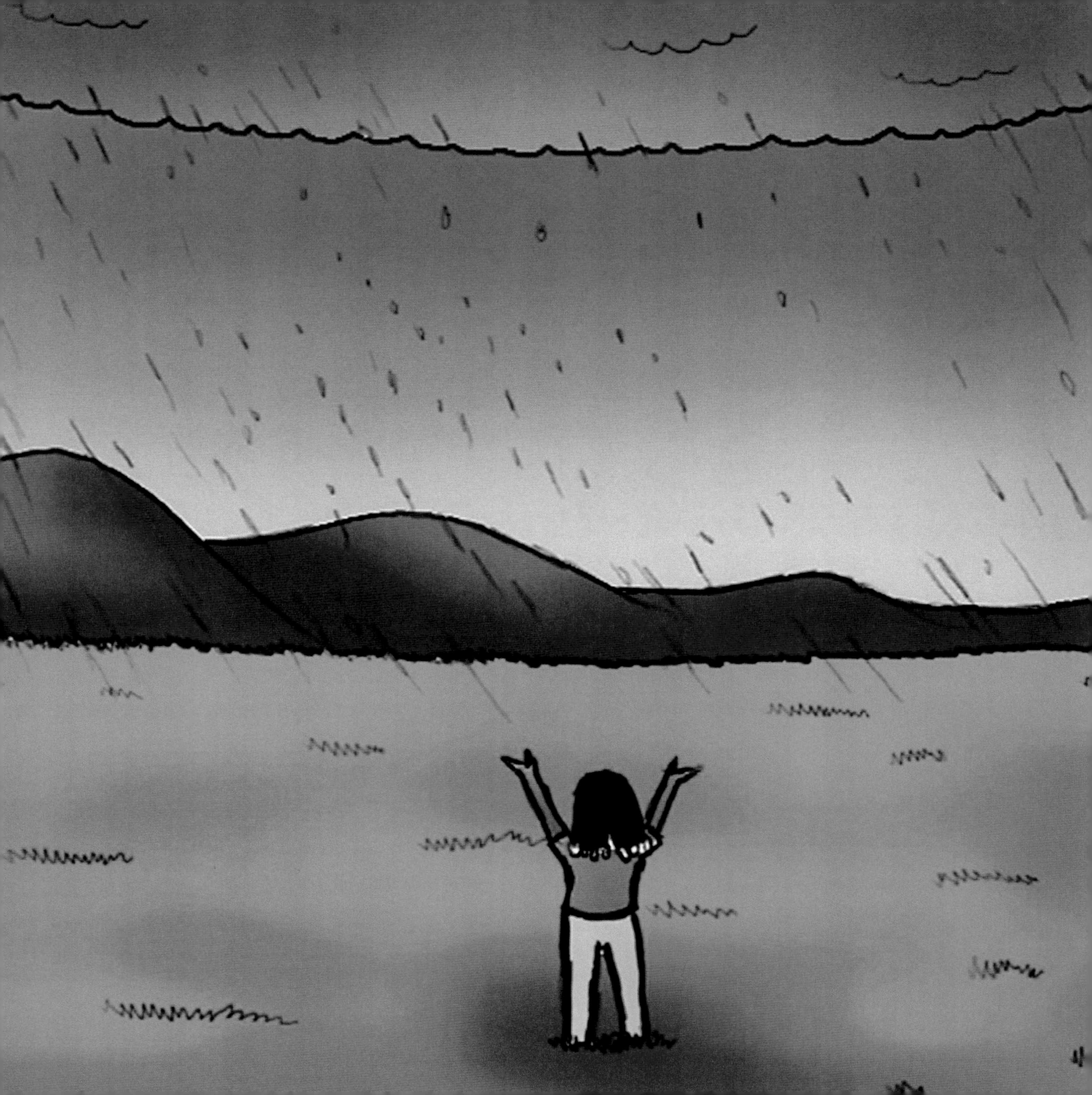

Cleanse the earth with your *Lovely* rain.

Now the flowers and food can grow.

Make the earth **happy**, clean, and whole.

Remind people to relax and breath.

I shall get my cup of chamomile tea.

As I watch you dance so gracefully!

Rain, rain don't go away. We are always **happy** when you stay.

<u>About *Rain Please Stay*</u>

This book was inspired by NATURE.

People often wish the rain away, however; they don't realize that without the rain most of our beautiful planet would be like a desert!

The next time you see rain remember to be grateful.

Who Is *TefNut..?*

--TefNut--

TefNut (rain) is an aspect of Nature. In ancient Kemet (Egypt), TefNut was depicted with the head of a lioness sitting on a throne. TefNut is moisture, dew, and rain. She is the companion of Shu (air).

Fun Facts About The Rain

We all know that rain is good for our planet; it gives us fresh water to drink, helps farmers grow crops, keeps everything green and lush, and it is fun to run around in.

Let's take a journey and learn all about the rain!

What Is Rain?

Rain is actually part of a bigger part of the weather called precipitation, which is any form of water that falls to the earth like rain, snow, drizzle, hail, and sleet.

How Is Rain Formed?

Water is always moving; rain that has fallen where you live may have been water in the ocean a couple of days before.

Water can be in the atmosphere, on land, in the ocean, and even underground. It gets used repeatedly through what is called the water cycle. Yayyy, for the water cycle! In this cycle water changes from liquid, to solid and to gas (which is water vapor.)

The water vapor then gets into the atmosphere through a process called evaporation. This then turns the water that is at the top of oceans, rivers, and lakes into water vapor in the atmosphere using energy from the sun. This vapor can also form snow and ice too.

The water vapor rises in the atmosphere, and there it cools down and forms tiny water droplets through something called condensation. These then turn into clouds. When they all combine, they grow bigger and are too heavy to stay up in the air.   This is when they will fall to the ground as rain, snow, or hail because of gravity.

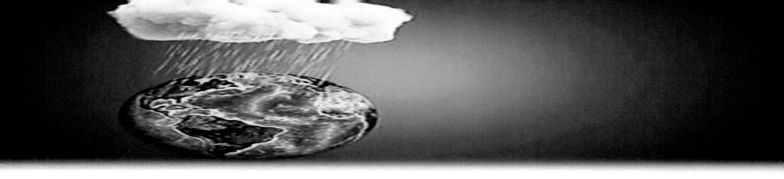

What Happens To Rain As It Falls?

Once the rain has fallen, a lot of it goes into oceans, rivers, lakes, and streams that will all eventually lead to our oceans. Snow and ice stay on the surface of the earth, like glaciers and other types of ice. Some rain seeps into the ground.

Fun Facts About Rain.

- Water stays in some places longer than others. A drop of water may spend over 3,000 years in the ocean before moving on to another part of the water cycle. Wow! On average a drop of water spends about 8 days in the atmosphere before falling back down to Earth.
- The highest amount of rainfall recorded in one year was 1,000 inches in Cherrapunji, India. That is a lot of rain.
- Antarctica is the driest continent on Earth.
- Raindrops fall at a speed of 1 to 18 mph. When there is wind, they could fall much faster.
- Do you think rain is just water? Well, it's not. It can have all sorts of things in it like dirt, dust, insects, grass, or even chemicals. It is not a good idea to swallow rain.

Vocabulary

Precipitation – any form of water that falls to the Earth.

Atmosphere – a thin layer of gases that surround the Earth.

Condensation – this is when water vapor in the air goes from a gas back to a liquid and leaves the atmosphere, coming back down to the surface of the Earth.

Vapor – a gas.

A Message From Healing Blue Lotus Kids

"The rain helps me to relax and sleep better."

-Maya Foxx

"The rain is beautiful and sparkly."

-Nia Henry

"I Love you rain!"

-Kiya Henry

Let's sing a song about the rain.

Rain Please Stay

by HetHeru AnkhBaRa

- available now on CD.

Lyrics PLEASE...

One, two, three hit it!!

Rain, rain don't go away.
Please, please, please stay.
For as long as you can.

You cool me down,
on a hot summer day.

Cleanse the earth,
with your lovely rain.

Now the flowers and food can grow.
Make the earth happy,
clean and whole.

Remind people to relax
and breath.
I shall get my cup of chamomile tea.

As I watch you dance
so gracefully.
Rain, rain don't go away.
We are always happy
when...you stay.

Made in the USA
Middletown, DE
05 November 2022

14182484R00022